FORTUNE

DIANE STANLEY

MORROW JUNIOR BOOKS
NEW YORK

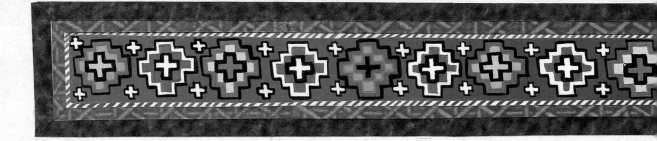

Printed in Hong Kong at South China Printing Company (1988) Ltd.
1 2 3 4 5 6 7 8 9 10

Library of Congress Cataloging-in-Publication Data
Stanley, Diane
Fortune.
Summary: In long ago Persia a poor young man,
following the advice of his betrothed, goes to the
city to seek his fortune and finds it in an unexpected
way.
[1. Fairy tales. 2. Tigers—Fiction] I. Title.
PZ8.S483Fo 1989 [E] 88-13204
ISBN 0-688-07210-0
ISBN 0-688-07211-9 (lib. bdg.)

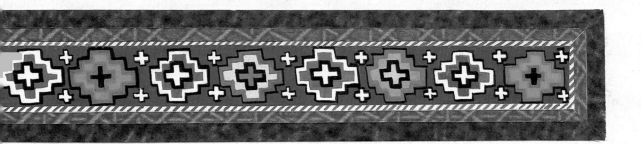

for

TAMARA

who helped me

Long ago, in the poorest corner of Persia, there lived a farmer and his son, whose name was Omar. When Omar came of age, all his father could give him were his blessing and a small purseful of money. With that he would have to make his way in the world, but poor Omar had no idea what to do or where to go.

Now, as a young boy, Omar had been betrothed to a girl from a neighboring farm whose name was Sunny. She was cheerful and hardworking, with bright eyes and a delightful way of laughing. Sunny's hair often lay as the wind blew it, and her apron was seldom clean, which was not so strange for a farmer's daughter. Omar and Sunny had been loving friends from childhood, and he was not bothered by her country ways. He was, after all, a farmer's son.

And so, in this great hour of decision, Omar went to Sunny for advice. For if he could not find a way to make a living, they would remain unmarried until their hair was as white as snow.

Sunny thought it over for a little while.

"It seems to me," she said at last, "that the place to seek your fortune is wherever people gather to do business. Go to the market town—and keep your eyes open!"

Omar took this good advice. When he reached the market town, he was amazed. Such crowds! Such noise! Such riches! Surely fortune lies here somewhere, he thought, if only I can figure out where. And he sat down to rest, for he was hot and tired.

"You there, young man!" called a voice from the crowd. "I have what you need, if you will but come here and look!"

The voice was a woman's, but the speaker was so wrapped in scarves and shawls that Omar could not guess her age or true appearance. She was pointing to a large and beautiful tiger curled in the dust at her feet.

"May Allah protect me!" cried Omar. "This is *not* what I need!"

The voice laughed from the scarves and shawls. "Don't be a fool. It is as tame as a lamb, and clever besides. If I play

this little pipe, it will dance." And with that she blew some soft, reedy notes and the great creature rose up, with sad eyes, and began to dance on its hind legs.

"Put this little hat on its head," said the woman with a nasty chuckle, "and take it from town to town. People will pay to see it dance. I tell you again, young man, this is surely what you need!"

"Whether I need it or not," said Omar, "I have no money to pay for it."

"Oh? And what is in that purse you are holding? Cabbages?"

"It is money, but not enough to buy a tiger."

"As a matter of fact," said the woman, "your purse holds exactly enough, for I will give it to you for whatever you have."

Omar could not say no. Within minutes he was in the town square with his tiger, playing a shy little tune while the tiger swayed solemnly on its hind legs and the townspeople threw coins at their feet. Ah, Sunny was right, he thought. For a clever young man like myself, fortune awaits.

Sure enough, everywhere he went with his tiger he was showered with money. And with the beast curled up beside him at night, he never feared robbers. That is why he named his tiger Fortune.

Before he was a year older, Omar returned to his village a rich man. He had a fine house built for himself and spent his days at ease, sleeping when he liked and thinking what to do next.

It was clear that he should marry, yet Omar kept putting it off. Sunny was a delightful girl, it was true. She was sweet-natured and dependable. But now that he was a rich man, Omar felt he deserved a grander wife: a princess, perhaps, who smelled of cloves and jasmine and wore silks and had skin as soft as a flower petal.

And so he went to Sunny to release her from her promise. "You are a fine friend," he said, meaning to be kind. "You are not ugly, but you are not pretty, either. You are a farmer's daughter, you see, and I am now a great man. I should probably marry a princess. I'm sure you can see that it can never work out between us."

And with that he left his village and his little friend Sunny, whose sad, dark eyes reminded him strangely of the tiger's, and went out into the world to find a bride, riding Fortune.

Omar let the tiger lead him wherever it wanted to go. After many days they came to a grand city completely surrounded by a high wall, behind which rose glittering towers. Like mountains the towers were to him, and their roofs were formed in beautiful shapes, each one different from the others, and they shone in the sun like gold. Once he passed through the gate, which was as tall as a house, he saw that the

streets were not of dirt, but of colored stones laid out in delicate patterns, and, like the towers, each was different.

In the center of this splendid city stood a great palace. It had eight domes and more than a hundred windows. A grand staircase, both very long and very wide, was at its entrance. Omar was breathless at the sight of such wealth and beauty.

That evening, as he took his dinner in a tavern, he asked the serving woman about the great palace and who lived there.

"Oh, good sir, that belongs to the sultan Hadi Mufad and his daughter, Shirin, the weeping princess. Everyone knows that!"

"Why does she weep," asked Omar, "when she lives in such a magnificent palace and in such a beautiful city?"

"She weeps for her prince, who is lost to her," answered the servant. "Everyone knows that, too."

"Not everyone knows these things," said Omar. "Please tell me about the weeping princess. I have my reasons for asking."

And when he had given the servant a cup of wine to wet her lips and some money to loosen her tongue, she told him this story:

There once lived a great king who had one son. The king desired to find a suitable bride for the young prince, and messengers were sent to a neighboring ruler who had a daughter of about the same age. The parents came to an agreement without much fuss and bother, so the prince, still crawling about in the garden and putting pebbles into his mouth, was promised in marriage to a princess who was crying in her cradle.

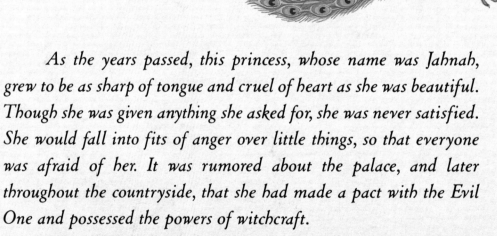

As the years passed, this princess, whose name was Jahnah, grew to be as sharp of tongue and cruel of heart as she was beautiful. Though she was given anything she asked for, she was never satisfied. She would fall into fits of anger over little things, so that everyone was afraid of her. It was rumored about the palace, and later throughout the countryside, that she had made a pact with the Evil One and possessed the powers of witchcraft.

The prince, who had never met his bride-to-be, had heard these stories and was worried. But when she arrived for the wedding and he saw how wicked she really was, he knew that he must escape from this hateful marriage. So he fled his father's palace in terror.

He went far, far away, and arrived at last at this same fair city. Here he met the princess Shirin, whose kindness and beauty touched his heart. The sultan saw that his daughter loved the noble stranger as she loved her own life, and so he gave his blessing.

The day before the wedding was to take place, the prince vanished. His horse was found tethered to a tree by the river, where he had gone to swim. Most people said he had drowned, but some believed he had been enchanted by a witch.

Finishing her wine, the servant girl said she was of the second opinion.

Omar's mind was so inflamed by this story that he could not sleep. He was convinced it was fate that he should have this princess for his wife. Had not Fortune led him here? Surely Fortune would carry him to the completion of his destiny!

That night, having come up with no better plan, Omar rode directly to the palace. He clutched Fortune tightly as they made their way up the broad staircase to the entrance.

There were guards everywhere, of course, but they all drew back at the first sight of the tiger, and let them pass, as if by magic. At last they came to a steep staircase lit only by shafts of moonlight through narrow windows in the wall. Leaving the tiger below, Omar climbed in the cool darkness until he came to a door. He opened it.

What he saw inside took his breath away. Lying in moonlight and shadow, curled upon a silk couch, was a young girl whose tear-stained face was as simple as a child's and as radiant as an angel's.

"Oh, stars in heaven!" exclaimed Omar, when he found his voice. "If I could gaze upon that face every morning I would always be happy!"

But what if the princess should not wish to follow him back to his farm and be his wife? That was a problem.

Though I am a handsome fellow, and rich enough, thought Omar, princesses have a way of wanting to marry

princes, and this one seems to have her heart set on a lost
cause.

Perhaps he could trick her into riding away with him.
Once she got to know him, she would surely forget her
beloved prince, since the prince was gone and Omar would be
there before her eyes.

He woke the princess and whispered softly to her, "I
have come to take you to your prince."

Without any questions or hesitation, the princess rose
and followed him down the dark staircase.

This is encouraging! thought Omar as they descended.

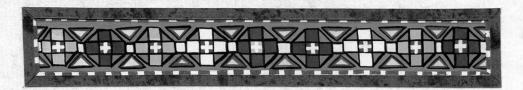

When she saw the tiger, however, she recoiled in fear, but he calmed her by saying, "The beast is tame. He will take you to your prince."

"If so, then he is my dearest friend," she said with emotion, "and I shall gladly embrace him!" And with these words she clasped her arms around the neck of the tiger.

Suddenly there was a roar like a great thunderclap and a blinding light. Omar fell to the ground, covering his face and trembling with fear. In a moment it was over, and, looking up, he saw the princess in the arms of a richly dressed youth. Of his tiger, nothing remained but the collar, lying on the ground.

Although Omar had meant only to tell a little lie when he had promised to bring the princess to her prince, he had in fact told the truth. For the wicked Jahnah had indeed worked an enchantment upon the prince. Not only had she changed him into a tiger, but she had also led him far away to a poor town in a forgotten corner of the country. There she had spitefully sold him to the simple-looking Omar, expecting that he would spend the remainder of his life dancing in the dust of dirty villages, wearing a silly hat. Nothing could break his enchantment but the embrace of the princess Shirin, which, considering the distance to her city and the general feeling of princesses for tigers, was an unlikely occurrence. But Jahnah, who had never known love, did not know its power to overcome even the greatest hardships.

The wedding of the prince and princess was celebrated with unimaginable splendor. There was no more sadness and no more weeping in their days. They lived a long life together and knew the joy of having many healthy children.

No one knows what became of the wicked Jahnah. It was said that, when she heard her enchantment was undone, she threw such a fit of anger that she died of it. This may or may not be true, but she never bothered anyone again.

As for Omar, everyone believed he had meant to bring the prince and princess together again. He was relieved to keep his foolishness to himself. The sultan made him a nobleman and gave him great lands and a splendid house and more wealth than he could ever spend. And so, for the second time, Omar's fortune was made, and he went off in search of that which would make his happiness complete.

Omar returned to his village and to the house of his neighbor, the farmer. There he found Sunny spinning in the courtyard.

"So, Omar," she teased when she saw him, "have you married a princess yet?"

Poor Omar told the whole story and confessed what a fool he had been for forgetting his friends and thinking himself so grand. "Oh, Sunny," he moaned, "what I would give if you would still see fit to be my wife!"

"Well," said Sunny, "I don't know. You're not ugly, but you're not handsome, either. And you're certainly not a prince."

Omar blushed with shame.

"But, on the other hand," she added, "I'm not a princess, and you have always been my treasured friend. Yes, I'll marry you." And she laughed her silvery laugh.

And so they were married. They, too, had many children and lived a long life together. In truth, though it is hard to be certain about such things, they were probably just as happy as the prince and princess.